The Friendship Book

Mary Lyn Ray

Illustrated by Stephanie Graegin

Houghton Mifflin Harcourt
Boston   New York

For my very first friends, Sharon and Kathy
and a dog named Snowball —M.L.R.

For my best friend, Gloria —S.G.

hmhbooks.com

The illustrations in this book were done in pencil
and watercolor and assembled and colored digitally.
The text type was set in Adobe Caslon Pro.
Hand lettering by Leah Palmer Preiss

Library of Congress Cataloging-in-Publication
Data is on file.

ISBN: 978-1-328-48899-2

Manufactured in China
SCP 10 9 8 7 6 5 4 3 2 1
4500773044

Sometimes being friends begins all at once.

And sometimes it takes awhile
to get acquainted.

But then, as some small knowing
grows, you start feeling that feeling
that comes with having a friend—

as if there's sunshine in your pocket
or inside you.

A friend is someone you like to be with,
and they like being with you.

A friend is to sit with,

do things with,

make wishes with,

and just be quiet with.

Friends share their secret wonderings

and their secret places.

They share lunches

and stories

and can't-hold-them-in laughs.

A friend can seem exactly like you.
Then you don't really have to ask
"Do you—?" or say "Me too! Me too!"

because, from the start, you almost
knew *something* made you the same.

Or a friend may seem very different at first.

But once you're friends, what matters is ~~inviting~~ friends.

Friends don't have to be alike in every way.
Or have to always agree.

And sometimes they get mad.

But it doesn't last.

Because they're friends.

When you get to know a friend,
you can tell how they are feeling.

So if you see they need some extra sunshine,
you reach into your pocket and say "Here."

Or maybe you say nothing. You're just there.

That can be enough when you're friends.

A best thing about a friend is being together.

But if friends must be far apart,
they don't forget each other.

And that makes far away feel smaller.

There are old friends and new friends

and always room for more friends.

When you don't have a friend, you wish you did.

Then it can help to remember
that a tree can be a friend.
So can a rock you like to sit on
or a lake or pond or grassy hill
or some green mossy place.

A dog or cat

or nuzzly horse can, too.

And somewhere there's someone
who's also waiting to be your friend—

the way you're waiting to be theirs.

Anyone might be a friend—

you just don't know yet.

And even though you can never tell
when a friend will happen,
being friends could begin when
you say "Hello."